Brooklynn, The Littlest Unicorn

The Adventure Begins

Alvin Walker

ISBN: 978-1-7378051-0-6 (Digital online)
ISBN: 978-1-7378051-1-3 (Paperback)
ISBN: 978-1-7378051-2-0 (Hardcover)

Library of Congress Control Number: 2021917247
Walker, Alvin

Any references to historical events, real people, or real places are used fictitiously. Names, characters, and places are products of the author's imagination.

Front cover image by Endless_exp
Images by Endless_exp

Printed in the United States of America.

First printing edition 2021.

Publisher by Alvin Walker
Contact Info: https://www.amazon.com/author/alvinwalker.com

My Book

My Name: _____

My Address _____

My Phone Number _____

Love You, Linda

Dedication

This wonderful child's book is dedicated to my late sister, Linda. Rest in peace, you will be missed.

Thank you,
Alvin Walker

Table of Content

About Author

Hello, my name is Alvin Walker. I am a simple man that loves his kids and grandchildren. I have spent much of my time with my grandkids traveling, fishing, riding horses and flying drones. During our time together, I noticed the unusual ways they socialize with others and the different personalities they develop through life experiences.

Introduction

In a faraway distant land where toadstools are as big as trees and beautiful flowers are everywhere, with a rainbow covering the entire sky, there lived a little unicorn named Brooklynn. She lived there with her family and friends. A place where young unicorns can run in fields of flowers under a rainbow sky.

Chapter 1: About Brooklynn

Brooklynn was the littlest unicorn in the family and the community of unicorns, she was the baby unicorn. There was a father unicorn. He was large and strong. Her mother was very caring and sweet. Her brother was nice to her sometimes and sometimes not so nice.

Chapter 2: Brooklynn and the other Unicorns

Brooklynn felt sorry about being so little and no one wanting her around. Go away," they said. "You will get us into trouble." This made Brooklynn incredibly sad.

"They always tell me what to do because I am so little My brother always picks on me because I am so small," Brooklynn said.

Chapter 3: Getting Ready for the Race

An event that all the young unicorns were practicing for was the great race. Brooklynn was no exception. She practiced daily because no one would run with her except her dad. Sometimes, she would beat him.

Brooklynn was amazingly fast, and nobody knew except her family. Brooklynn loved to run. It was her favorite thing to do. Brooklynn's dad was a runner when he was a young unicorn. She loved it when her dad chased her, and sometimes, he could not catch her.

Chapter 4: Day of the Race

The morning of the race, Brooklynn was incredibly happy but nervous about the race. Her mother and father talked to her about it. They told her no matter how small she is, she matters. If she did her best and did not give up, they would be proud of her no matter if she won or lost. This lifted Brooklynn's spirit, and she was ready!

"Girl power!" Brooklynn shouted.

Brooklynn and her family started their journey to the racing event at the bottom of the grand old toadstool. Brooklynn's brother teased her the whole way there.

He said, "You're too little to race. You're going to embarrass us." But Brooklynn did not believe that. She believed she was a giant.

Chapter 5: The Race

Brooklynn and her family finally reached the grand old toadstool, where everyone met them. There were unicorns and their families from other areas. After welcoming and greeting everyone, they all had a bite to eat. There were about twenty racers. They were all varied sizes, from small to large. Brooklynn was the smallest unicorn in the race. After they got through welcoming and greeting everyone, it was time for the racers to get ready. Down by the grand old toadstool, everyone lined up next to each other behind the tape. Brooklynn was on the end, so she would not get lost among the other racers. The race was from the grand old toadstool to the creek and back. The leader of the unicorns said get ready. The racers got ready. "Go!"

When the racers started, they caused so much fairy dust you could not see anything. When the dust cleared, Brooklynn was still there. The crowd said, "Aww." She could not see which way to go. But when she saw the racers, they were out in front. Brooklynn took off like lightning, shouting, "Girl power!"

Brooklynn caught up with the others in a brief time. Everyone was cheering for Brooklynn. Brooklynn's parents were so proud. When the racers got closer to the creek, they blocked Brooklynn from getting out in front. Brooklynn was so small she ran through the other unicorn's legs and came out in front. "Way to go," Brooklynn's brother said. Brooklynn reached the creek, and the other unicorns were right behind her.

The crowd was cheering louder and louder. Brooklynn's spirit soared as she put on speed. Brooklynn and other racers head back toward the grand old toadstool with her in the lead.

Brooklynn's brother shouted, "That's my sister!"

All the other unicorns in the race were giving their best and a couple started getting closer to Brooklynn. Brooklynn's parents shouted, "Come on, Brooklynn, you can do it! That's our daughter!"

At that time, the other unicorn racers were at Brooklynn's heels, so she imagined her dad chasing her. Brooklynn got a happy feeling from inside. Brooklynn shouted, "Girl power!" And she shot across the finish line.

The crowd yelled, "Yay! Brooklynn!" Everyone ran toward her, including her parents and brother. Brooklynn's parents hugged her and told her how proud they were of her. Her brother said, "You did alright." Brooklynn was so happy.

The Conclusion

After the big race, life was completely different for Brooklynn. The other young unicorns invited her to play. Everyone welcomed her around. Her brother treated her better. He stopped saying terrible things about her. She was invited to lots of parties.

Brooklynn made a lot of friends. Life was good for Brooklynn.

The End

Bye

www.ingramcontent.com/pod-product-compliance
Lightning Source LLC
Chambersburg PA
CBHW041609120626
46551CB00002B/374